Garden pavilion and vegetable garden as seen from Mulberry Row. LEF

East front. THOMAS JEFFERSON MEMORIAL FOUNDATION, INC./ JAMES TKATCH

MONTICELLO

Leonard Everett Fisher

Holiday House / New York

The West Front, a watercolor by Jane Bradick, 1825/1826. Depicted
are Jefferson's grandchildren and the artist's brother.

West front.　THOMAS JEFFERSON MEMORIAL FOUNDATION, INC./ JAMES TKATCH

"I am as happy nowhere else and in no other society, and all my wishes end, where I hope my days will end, at Monticello," wrote Thomas Jefferson while in France following the American Revolution. Mr. Jefferson had already written the Declaration of Independence in 1776. And he had been governor of Virginia. Now he was living in Paris, where he represented the new government of the United States of America. An ocean away from home, he continued to think of his dream house—Monticello—"little mountain." The house, still unfinished, had been under construction for about fifteen years.

Jefferson, now a widower, busied himself with official matters. His wife of ten years, Martha Wayles Skelton, had died. But the more he worked and traveled in Europe, the more he longed for the home on his little mountain; for his family and friends; for the peacefulness of his gardens away from the noise of civilization and the commotion of politics. He would have to wait five years in France, making treaties and winning new friends for the United States, before he could set eyes once more on the soft, rolling landscape of his native Virginia. Not until George Washington became the first president of the United States and appointed Thomas Jefferson his secretary of state would the tall, lanky, red-headed architect of Monticello go home. And he would have to wait still another twenty years before he could rid himself of politics and retire to "... the bosom of my family ... surrounded by my books ... [enjoying] a repose to which I have been long a stranger."

Creating a building crept into Jefferson's mind early in his busy and distinguished life while he was still a student at William and Mary College in Williamsburg, Virginia. Young Jefferson found the style of Williamsburg's Georgian brick mansions and wooden frame homes ordinary. They were a good deal less magnificent than the architecture of ancient Greece and Rome whose spectacular buildings befitted the grandeur of their civilizations.

At William and Mary College, Jefferson bought a book on architectural design. And from that moment on, he indulged a growing passion for architecture. It would endure his entire life.

Architecture, as a profession, did not exist in colonial America. There were no "architects," as such. Not from the time of the founding of Jamestown, Virginia, in May 1607 until the coming of Thomas Jefferson—a spread of more than one hundred years—was there anyone professional planning or designing buildings for a specific purpose. Neither was there a recognized school or profession of architecture in England during the seventeenth century. Inigo Jones (1573–1652) and Christopher Wren (1632–1723), the two men most responsible for the design and appearance of many of England's important public buildings during the seventeenth century, were not trained architects.

Jones began his career as a painter and scene designer for the royal theater. His interest in brush, canvas, and the theater took him to Italy. There he fell under the spell of the stately palaces designed by the sixteenth century Italian architect Andrea Palladio (1518–1580). Palladio had carefully studied the architectural styles of ancient Rome, which in turn were largely influenced by the earlier civilization of Greece. Palladio's designs, based on the structures of ancient Greece and Rome, became known as the "Palladian" style. Jones gave up his painting ambitions and returned to England, bringing with him enthusiasm for Palladian architecture. He was appointed royal surveyor to King James I and began to

A bust of Thomas Jefferson by Jean-Antoine Houdon (1741–1828).

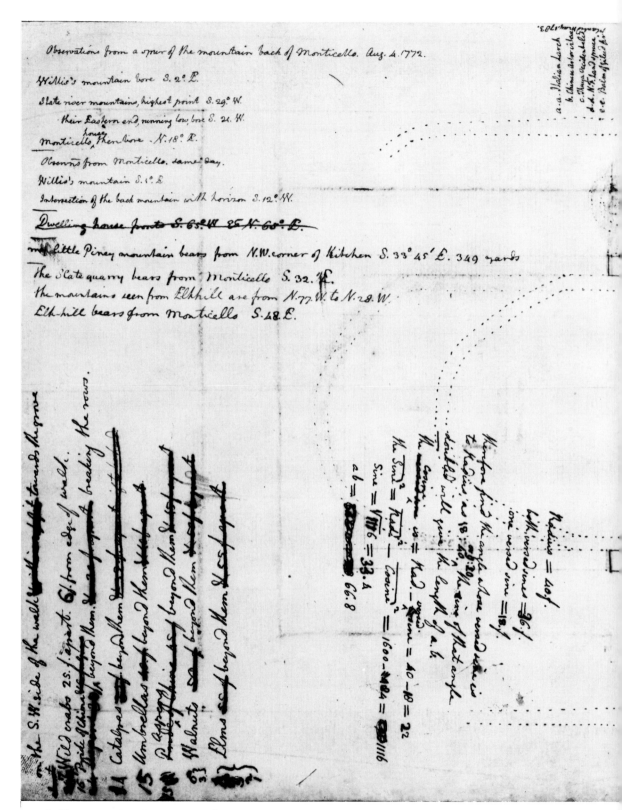

Jefferson's plan for the Monticello grounds. The drawing, begun in 1768, was annotated over the years.

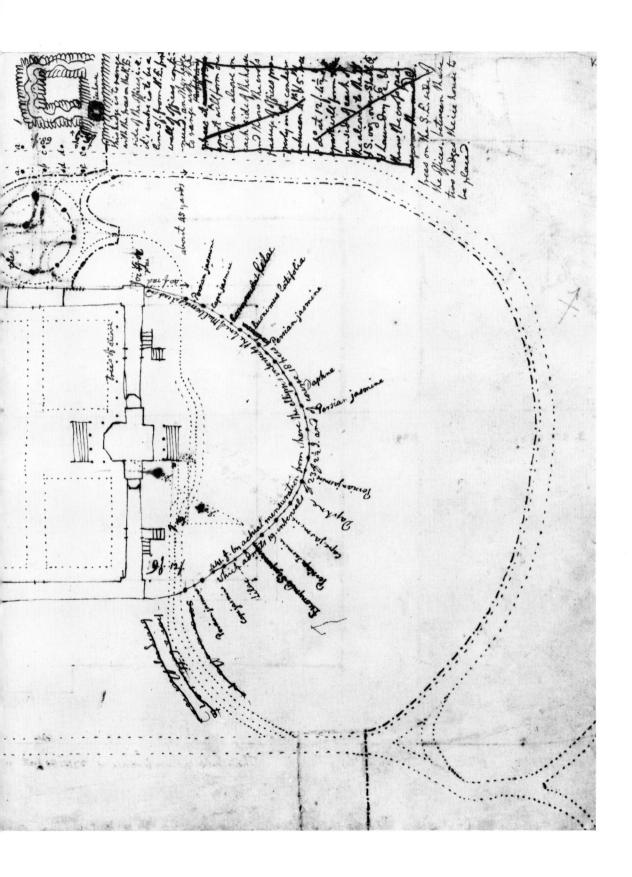

introduce the Palladian style to the construction of British public buildings.

Christopher Wren was a mathematician and astronomer. But like Jones, he, too, became royal surveyor by appointment to the court of King Charles II. When a great fire all but destroyed London in 1666, Wren was given the job of rebuilding the city. Wren had a sense of order and symmetry. He learned about building materials. He studied the architecture of classical Greece, Rome, and the more recent Renaissance designs of Italy, France, and Flanders. He was well aware of Palladio's influence on Inigo Jones. In the end, Wren was able to combine his knowledge, mathematical skills, and instinct to create buildings that echoed the then-current European styles. At the same time his designs remained English in feeling and expression.

The redesigning and rebuilding of London following the fire caused a lively interest in architecture. A host of pamphlets, manuals, and books described in words and pictures every aspect of designing and constructing a building. These publications presented not only the actual details of style, ornament, and construction, but "how-to-build" as well.

For the architectural scholar there were Palladio's own drawings in his *Four Books of Architecture,* first published in Italy in 1570. The books were translated into English in 1713. James Gibbs (1682–1754), an English architect, published a much sought-after volume called *A Book of Architecture.* In addition there was Robert Morris's *Select Architecture;* Stephen Primatt's *The City and Country Purchaser and Builder; The Art of House Carpentry* by Joseph Moxon; William Halfpenny's *The Modern Builder's Assistant;* Batty Langley's *Treasury of Designs;* and a variety of publications showing the drawings or designs of Inigo Jones, Christopher Wren, and others.

Plate 41, Book 2 of the *Architecture of Andrea Palladio* from *In Four Books,* Revis'd, Design'd and Published by Giacemo Leone, London 1715. The U-shaped design was used by Jefferson for Monticello.   COURTESY OF THE RARE BOOK DIVISION, UNIVERSITY OF VIRGINIA LIBRARY

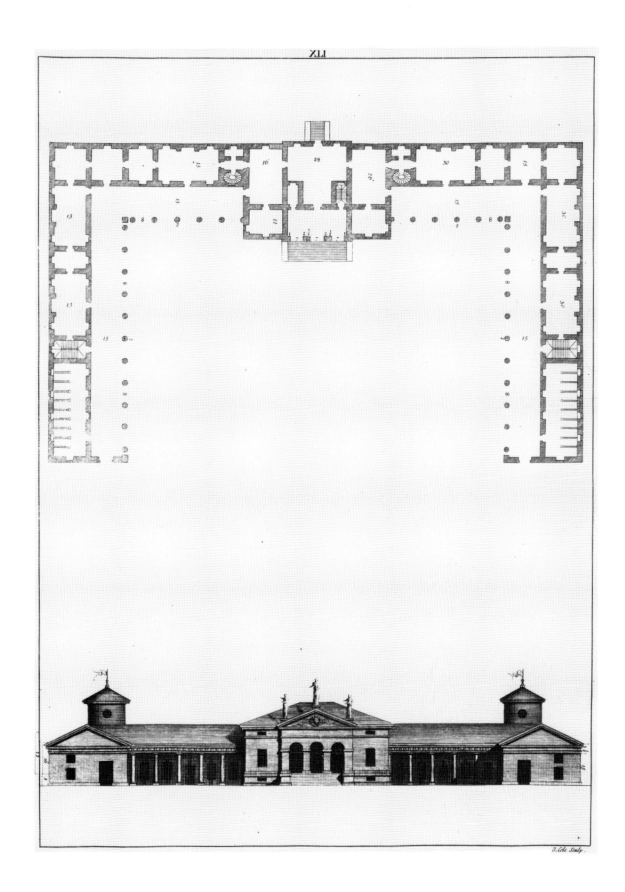

13

By the beginning of the eighteenth century and for the next forty or fifty years, droves of workmen skilled in the building trades and familiar with English and European architectural styles crossed the Atlantic Ocean seeking new opportunities in America. Many of them brought their work manuals and architectural books with them. These books, published in England, were soon seen in the private libraries of well-to-do colonists who used them to design new homes for themselves. They employed master builders and skilled workmen to see the jobs through. However, the ordinary shopkeeper, stone mason, tanner, papermaker, indentured servant, or slave could hardly read the books, let alone afford the luxury of building a house. So architectural planning only happened in the design of public buildings, private estates, plantation mansions, or stylish town houses.

Among wealthy gentlemen of the South, it was a badge of aristocratic status and education to be able to draw or paint "landskips," or landscapes, and to have some knowledge of architectural styles. Combining both these skills allowed the gentlemen farmers and merchants to create plans and pictures of their dream houses—to become, at best, amateur architects. The actual methods of construction were left to the master builders who were responsible for carrying out the ideas of the families who employed them. The master builder—the craftsman skilled in all of the building trades himself and familiar with style and books of design—in turn hired laboring craftsmen and supervised the entire construction process. It was the master builder in British America, north or south, with his wide knowledge of tools, materials, methods, style, engineering, and finishing details who would one day evolve into the professional architect.

Thomas Jefferson became his own master builder on land

inherited from his father, wealthy Peter Jefferson. The elder Jefferson had owned a thousand acres of Virginia land just east of the Blue Ridge Mountains. Eventually, the Jefferson land holdings would increase to five thousand acres. It was on these acres called "Shadwell" that Thomas Jefferson was born, April 13, 1743, the oldest son of ten children. Fourteen years later, Peter Jefferson died, leaving his entire estate, including more than twenty slaves, to Thomas and his younger brother Randolph. The tract included the little 867-foot wooded mountain where young Tom played and that he would one day call "Monticello."

Ten years later, in 1767, Jefferson, now a lawyer, decided to follow his dream of building a home on the mountaintop. This was an unheard of thing to do in colonial America, let alone in Virginia. There was no system of highways or of even lesser roads in early America that could make a mountaintop home easily reached. The usual and more practical thing to do was to build a home near a river, lake, or ocean. Water, especially rivers, was the chief highway system. Nevertheless, Jefferson thought of his mountaintop home as a retreat from which he would have a perfect view of the Virginia landscape he loved so much.

Work began in earnest the following year, 1768, when Jefferson leveled the mountaintop, creating a flat surface on which to build his house. Construction began in 1769, the same year Thomas Jefferson became the delegate from Albemarle County to Virginia's House of Burgesses in Williamsburg, the capital, some 110 miles southeast of Monticello. Now, not only would he be consumed by his passion for Monticello, he would slowly be drawn into the fight for American independence. The colonists did not want to be subjected to British laws that ignored their interests. They

View of Monticello, a watercolor by Cornelia J. Randolph, Jefferson's
granddaughter, 1868.   THOMAS JEFFERSON MEMORIAL FOUNDATION, INC.

16

C.J.B. 1868

17

wanted to be free to conduct their own affairs.

Jefferson set down on paper sketchy visions of the house and prepared mechanical working drawings—a skill that he had taught himself—for his craftsmen to follow. And Jefferson, always the supervisor, would permit not a hair's difference between the measurements on his working drawings and the actual construction. The basic materials needed for the initial construction were found in the area. Timber was taken from his own forests and dressed in a carpentry shop or "joinery" set up on the mountaintop. Stone blocks for the foundation were cut out of the mountain. Bricks were fired in Monticello's own mountaintop kiln. Obviously, some of the more intricate fittings such as brass locks and doorknobs or glass had to be made elsewhere. But again, Jefferson, the master builder, studied the crafts of stonecutting, brick making, and carpentry, then employed skilled craftsmen to carry out the work.

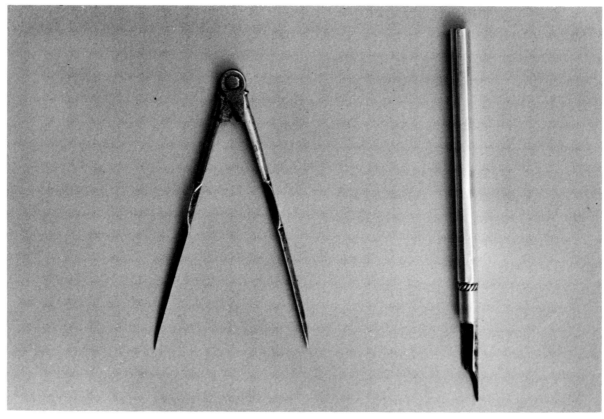

Jefferson's drawing tools.   THOMAS JEFFERSON MEMORIAL FOUNDATION, INC.

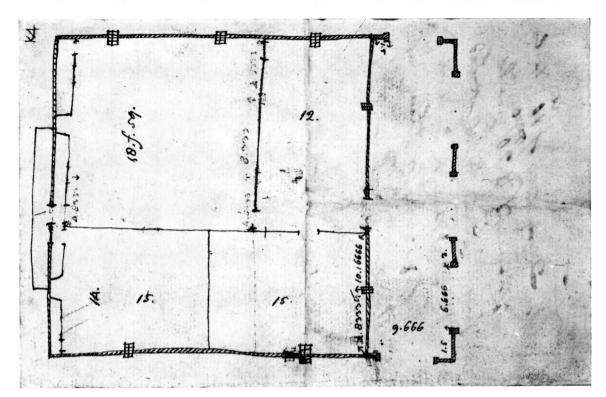

Jefferson's first plan of Monticello, 1767. MASSACHUSETTS HISTORICAL SOCIETY

Jefferson's sketch for the first version of Monticello, circa 1770.
THOMAS JEFFERSON MEMORIAL FOUNDATION, INC.

By 1770 a small brick building, the south pavilion, was finished. And none too soon! The Jefferson homestead at Shadwell had burned, leaving Jefferson without adequate housing. He immediately moved into the south pavilion and wrote, "I have . . . one room which, like a cobbler's, serves me for parlor . . . kitchen . . . hall . . . bedchamber and study. . . ." Meanwhile, farther to the north in Boston, Massachusetts, British troops fired into a protesting mob in front of the state house, killing four people. That event, the Boston Massacre, moved the American colonies a violent step toward independence from Great Britain. The future looked ominous. But work on Monticello never stopped.

The south pavilion was one of two like buildings. The other was the north pavilion, which was built later and served as an office-study for Thomas Jefferson's son-in-law, Thomas Mann Randolph. Both buildings were separate from the main house

South pavilion, 1987. LEF

but eventually connected to it by raised wood walkways or platforms called "terraces." Jefferson's master plan called for the terraces to roof over and hide from view the various service areas—"dependencies"—for the main house. Thus, beneath the south terrace were the south dependencies. These were used as slave quarters, the kitchen, and a smokehouse for curing and preserving meats. The north dependencies included stables, carriage houses, an icehouse, and a laundry. The plan made it possible for Jefferson's slaves, whom he usually called "servants," to be protected from any kind of weather as they came and went. These L-shaped terrace links between the main house and the north and south pavilions were not fully completed until after 1800.

As work progressed on the mountaintop, Jefferson found time to court Martha Wayles Skelton, a wealthy twenty-three-year-old widow. They were married near Williamsburg on

North pavilion, 1987. LEF

South terrace and south dependencies, circa 1940.

New Year's Day, January 1, 1772. The trip from Williamsburg to Monticello in a two-horse carriage began in a light snowfall that soon turned heavy. The journey was slow and almost had to end as the carriage broke down and was abandoned in the deep drifts. The couple finished the trip up the mountain on their unhitched horses.

Their arrival was unheralded. The only parts of the construction that were fully enclosed in January, 1772 were the finished south pavilion, Jefferson's living quarters, now sometimes referred to as the "honeymoon cottage," and possibly the mansion's dining room.

Between 1772 and 1782, construction crept along at a slow pace. A year after the newlyweds first moved into the south pavilion, work on the brick walls of the main house was still in progress. By the end of 1774 the center section of the mansion and its south wing had been completed and fourteen

Their arrival was unheralded. LEF

pairs of sash windows were on order. Also, a vegetable garden had been laid out on the southern slope below Mulberry Row. Mulberry Row was the working street of the estate where Jefferson had not only planted mulberries but had located the various craft shops used in the building and maintenance of Monticello.

What now emerged as an elegant building in Jefferson's grand design was a two-story home whose central section contained a front hall, parlor and upstairs library. Featured, too, was a double-decked portico or two colonnaded porches capped by a triangular pediment. As one entered the hall from the mansion's east front, the master bedroom was on the left, while the dining room was on the right. Passing from the hall directly into the parlor, a visitor would look out westward into the setting sun onto spacious grounds which ended at the south pavilion. The whole effect echoed versions of a building found in Robert Morris's 1755 book, *Select Architecture,* which borrowed from the work of Andrea Palladio. Palladio's sixteenth-century Villa Pisani served as Jefferson's model for the double-decked portico.

Meanwhile, the Jefferson family was growing. There would be six children. But only two would grow to adulthood, Martha Jefferson (1772–1836) and Mary Jefferson (1778–1804). Also, Jefferson was becoming increasingly more active in colonial-American politics. In 1774, while still a delegate to the Virginia House of Burgesses, he wrote *A Summary View of the Rights of British America* in which the power of England's Parliament over the American colonies was rejected. Later that year the First Continental Congress met in Philadelphia to decide America's course. It was not until May of the following year, as war with Britain exploded in Massachusetts, that Jefferson went to Philadelphia as a delegate to the Second

Villa Pisani, Italy, designed by Andrea Palladio,
16th century. JOSEPH FARBER

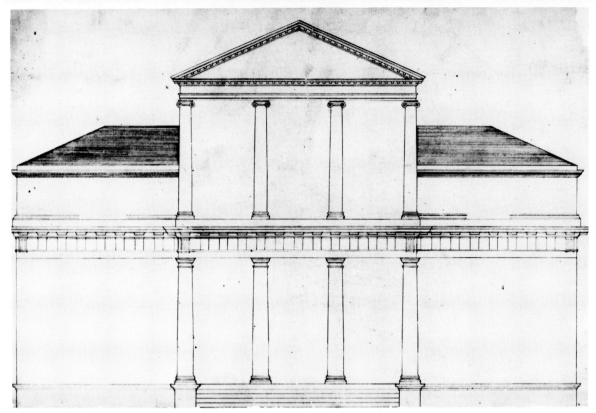

Jefferson's study for the first version of Monticello.

Jefferson's study for the first version of Monticello, 1771.

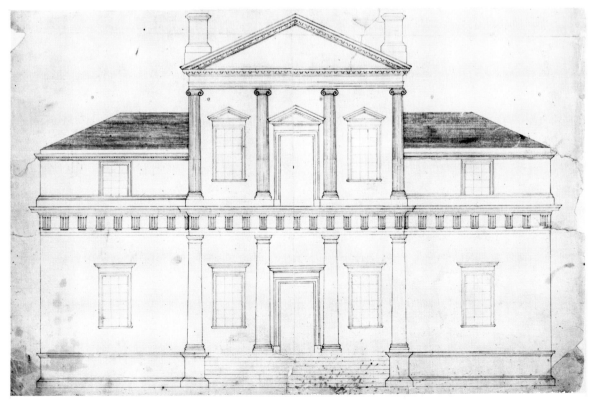

Continental Congress. Here he helped to write *The Declaration of Causes and Necessities of Taking Up Arms,* a document which explained why the colonists were willing to fight for their independence. A year later Jefferson authored the *Declaration of Independence,* which announced that all political connections between the colonies and Great Britain were dissolved.

Jefferson returned to Monticello in 1776 and then to Williamsburg to sit again as a delegate to the Virginia House of Burgesses. Three years later he gave up the seat to become governor of Virginia. All the while the War for Independence continued to a victorious end as the building of Monticello progressed toward its own splendid completion—but not without a scare.

With a large but doomed British army under Lord Charles Cornwallis roaming the Virginia countryside in 1781, Jefferson was hardly safe even on his mountaintop. With Richmond, now the capital of Virginia, in British hands, the enemy came looking for Governor Jefferson. But Jefferson and his family escaped to a friend's house. After spending the better part of a day at Monticello and drinking some of Jefferson's wine, the British cavalry troopers left. Luckily, there was no damage to any part of Monticello.

In 1782, the second of four roads—or second roundabout—encircling Monticello at various levels was finished. The first roundabout had been cut ten years earlier. The last of these roads would be built after 1800. Jefferson himself surveyed the terrain and supervised the construction of the roads. The roundabouts together with connecting paths made it easier to reach Monticello. They also provided the Jeffersons and their guests with walking and riding paths.

Also by 1782 Jefferson had devised a new plan for an old orchard that pre-dated the mansion. The plan called for an

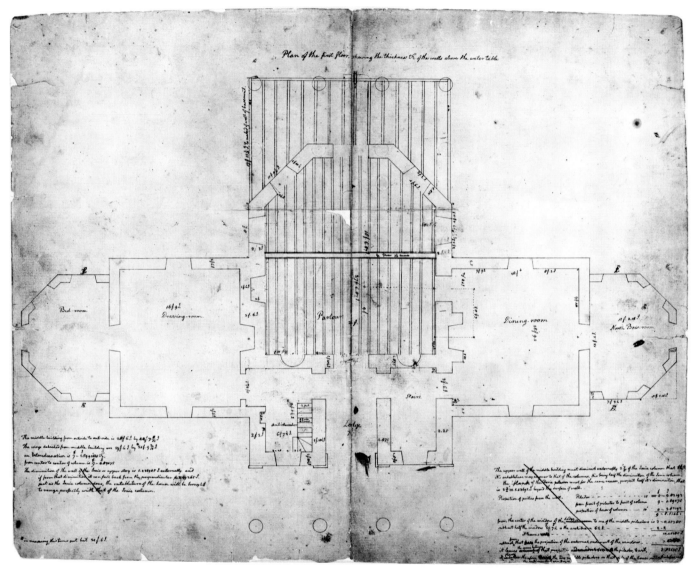

Jefferson's first floor plan for Monticello, circa 1771.
MASSACHUSETTS HISTORICAL SOCIETY

astonishing variety of fruit trees to be planted on the southern slope below the vegetable garden. In time the orchard would produce peaches, plums, apples, pears, cherries, apricots, nectarines, almonds, pecans, and more.

If Jefferson had any idea about spending his entire life with his family in the splendid isolation of their mountaintop, it was short-lived. As Lord Cornwallis was surrendering the British army to American forces in October, 1781, Jefferson's term as Virginia's governor had already come to an end. The thirty-eight-year-old Jefferson once again took up his seat in the House of Delegates, formerly the House of Burgesses, now located in Richmond, a good deal closer to Monticello than Williamsburg. Since the position required very little of his time, Jefferson spent most of his days with his wife and children at Monticello, planning and carrying out numerous projects. Unexpectedly, these happy days came to an abrupt end. Within a year his thirty-three-year-old wife died, leaving Jefferson griefstricken. But the distraught Jefferson had little time to mourn or care for his three daughters, one of whom died two years later. During 1783, he was asked to represent Virginia in the United States Congress. He did so for six months and recommended that the new country adopt a decimal monetary system with the dollar as its basic currency. He left the Congress in 1784 to represent the United States government as minister to France. There, in France, with his remaining two daughters, Mary and Martha, he spent the next five years pining away for the peace and beauty of his creation, Monticello. The estate itself was left in the care of a neighbor, Nicholas Lewis.

Jefferson did not waste his years in France with respect to his architectural enthusiasm. He spent a great deal of time studying buildings and gardens everywhere he traveled. He

Martha Jefferson Randolph by Thomas Sully (1783–1872).

also purchased a variety of furnishings for Monticello, including paintings, sculpture, linens, silver, and china.

There were a number of sights that Jefferson had seen in Europe that gave him pause about the appearance of Monticello. For one thing, country homes in America did not have to have multiple stories as did city houses. There was more space in the country than in a cramped city. City people had to build upward for lack of space. Country people had the space to spread outward. Suddenly, Jefferson saw little logic in Monticello's double-decked portico and lack of spread. A single portico would do. Monticello should reach outward not upward, and be larger. Also, Jefferson was attracted to the proportions and appearances of ancient classical buildings as well as new buildings in a way he had never been before. Now he was seeing them in actuality, not viewing them as pictures in a book. Among these buildings was the then eighteen-

Maison Carrée, Nimes, France, 1983. LEF

hundred-year-old Maison Carrée in Nimes in the south of France and the new Hôtel de Salm in Paris.

The ancient Maison Carrée, or Square House, is the best preserved of the old Roman temples. Planned with precisely arranged proportions of Greek origins, the Maison Carrée struck Jefferson as an ideally designed building. The stately colonnaded portico and its relationship to the rest of the structure became fixed in his mind. "Roman taste, genius, and magnificence excites ideas," he said. When asked to send a design for a capitol building in Richmond, Jefferson sent a sketch based on the Maison Carrée to "improve the taste of my countrymen, to increase their reputation, to reconcile to them the respect of the world and procure them its praise." What Jefferson foresaw and may have indeed generated was the notion that public buildings should have classical appearances. And that notion can be seen in much official American government architecture built during the nineteenth and early part of the twentieth centuries.

The other building that influenced Jefferson's architectural ideas when he lived in France was the Hôtel de Salm, under construction in 1785. It was a nobleman's one-story home surrounded by columns and topped by a dome. As elegant and stylish as it was comfortable and private, the Hôtel de Salm reflected the Palladian view of architecture and captured Jefferson's fascination. "I was violently smitten with the Hôtel de Salm," he wrote, "and used to go . . . almost daily to look at it."

A third building that caught Jefferson's interest was the domed and porticoed Roman Pantheon in the heart of Rome, the temple to all the gods. This building, so central to the life of Rome, was among those important buildings of classical times that inspired Palladio. Engravings of it inspired Jefferson to such an extent that he later used the Pantheon as the basis of his design for the rotunda of the University of Virginia, which he founded in 1819.

During his five-year stay in France, Jefferson toyed with the idea of making some alterations to Monticello. But when he returned home in November, 1789 to become President Washington's secretary of state, he decided to completely remodel his home. He thought it looked old-fashioned and clumsy, and out of step with what a modern country home should look like—low and uncrowded. "Architecture is my delight," he once said, "and putting up and pulling down, one of my favorite amusements."

Jefferson's new plan was to enlarge Monticello to have "all my rooms on one floor," making it seem to be a one-story home when in actuality there would be three floors; to pull down Monticello's upper portico, giving the entire structure a

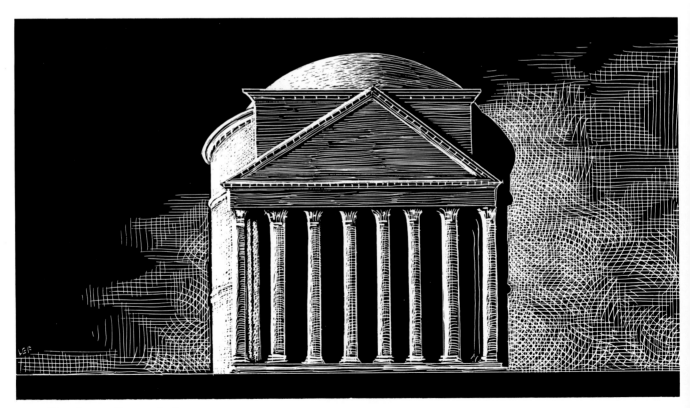

Pantheon, Rome, Italy. LEF

lower appearance; and to provide the center section of the building with a dome, the first on an American dwelling. The dome and colonnaded porch were among those outstanding architectural features that connected Jefferson to Palladio and to the classical building design.

Now busy as secretary of state, Jefferson spent most of his time in office feuding with New York's Alexander Hamilton over the interpretation of the Constitution. Jefferson, the southern Democratic-Republican, believed that ordinary people should have a voice in government; that America should base its well-being on farming; and that the states should have more control over their individual futures. Hamilton, the northern Federalist, believed in a strong central government; that America should base its well-being on manufacturing and banking; and that ordinary people should have no say in the government. The debate between the two later influenced America's two-party system. The Democratic party was modeled on Jefferson's position, the Republican party on Hamilton's. While debating Hamilton, Jefferson managed to find time to work on the mechanical drawings for the remodeling of Monticello. Finally, in 1796 the job of redoing the house began. It would take the next thirteen years to complete the remodeling.

The following year, 1797, Thomas Jefferson became President John Adams's vice-president. In the same year, Jefferson hired James Dinsmore, a skilled Philadelphia house builder, to oversee the project and speed things up. As Jefferson became more immersed in the country's politics and business—he succeeded Adams as third president of the United States in 1801—he hired several more highly skilled craftsmen for the Monticello alteration. By this time bricklayers had slowly established the new walls of the house. The mansion had been enclosed, the plastering of the walls had begun, and the dome had been constructed. In 1805, painters started a four-year job of painting Monticello's interior and wood exterior parts such as window frames and doors. The entire remodeling was completed in 1809, the year Jefferson finally stepped down from his presidential office and into his Monticello retirement.

The new appearance of Monticello in 1809 was substantially the mansion as it is known today. A visitor entering the entrance hall from the east portico would find a large room with a second floor balcony and no grand staircase. Jefferson had little use for staircases other than as access to upper or lower floors. In his mind grand and wide staircases took up too much room. Jefferson wanted to use all the space he could to exhibit his collection of Indian artifacts and natural history such as antlers, a buffalo head, and mastodon tusks. In keeping with his belief that space should be used economically, he hid two very narrow staircases—each twenty-four inches wide—in the north and south passages, the hallways of the north and south wings of the house. These led to the six rooms and the hall of the second floor. The rooms were used for storage, staff bedrooms, and a nursery for a grandchild. Staircases continued to a third floor having three skylighted, unheated bedrooms and the eight-sided dome room that seemed to serve as a children's playroom and at times a storeroom and an extra bedroom. This third floor was designed to be almost invisible when viewing the mansion from the outside.

The real life of the house took place in and around the grounds, including the north and south dependencies, and on the first floor.

The much-used parlor boasted one of the first parquet

Monticello entrance hall, looking toward the parlor.

Monticello entrance hall, looking toward the east entry.

Monticello dome room after restoration, 1984.

floors in America—a floor set in a pattern of highly polished hardwoods. It was separated from the entrance hall by twin glass doors that were semiautomatic. The movement of one door opened or closed the other. The mechanism was hidden beneath the floor.

Jefferson liked to create practical gadgets. Over the main entry doors of the entrance hall, he placed an hour clock connected to a seven-day calendar run by weights. The weights moved with the clock's ticking and controlled the gong on the roof that struck hourly. The days of the week were indicated by the movement of the weights, which passed by marks on the wall for Sunday through Friday. Since there was no room for Saturday, it was marked on the basement wall directly underneath. The clock's cable and weights ran through the floor into the basement. Another one of Jefferson's devices was the wind direction indicator that poked

The parlor's mechanical doors, circa 1930.

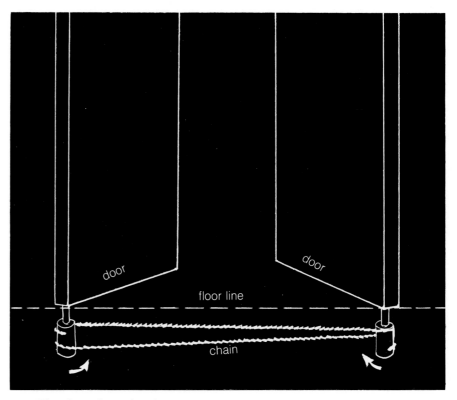

The doors' mechanism. LEF

Parlor.   THOMAS JEFFERSON MEMORIAL FOUNDATION, INC./ JAMES TKATCH

Dining Room.   THOMAS JEFFERSON MEMORIAL FOUNDATION, INC./ JAMES TKATCH through the ceiling of the east portico and was connected to a weathervane on the roof.

It was in the parlor that Jefferson arranged most of the French art he bought during his years as the American minister to France. Here, too, the Jefferson family celebrated their marriages, christenings, and conducted their musical concerts. A door from the parlor led into the dining room where double sliding doors opened into the tearoom. There were two additional doors in the dining room. One led directly to the entrance hall; the other to the north passage. Jefferson showed his imaginative streak in the dining room, too. On either side of the fireplace mantel were "dumb-waiters." These were mechanical lifts for sending wine bottles up from the cellar beneath. Also, there was a revolving door with shelves for holding dishes. Food placed on the door shelves on the pantry side appeared on the dining-room side

The dumbwaiter. LEF

44

Tearoom. THOMAS JEFFERSON MEMORIAL FOUNDATION, INC./ JAMES TKATCH

Wine room.   THOMAS JEFFERSON MEMORIAL FOUNDATION, INC./ JAMES TKATCH

Kitchen. THOMAS JEFFERSON MEMORIAL FOUNDATION, INC./ JAMES TKATCH

when the door was turned.

Jefferson's bedroom, library, and study were all in the south wing of the first floor. His bed separated the bedroom and the study. This way he could step from his bed into either room. Next to his study was his six-thousand-volume library. Jefferson sold his books to the government in 1815 to pay his mounting bills. The government used the collection to form the Library of Congress.

Other rooms on the first floor were the south piazza, a glass-enclosed porch that Jefferson used as a workshop and greenhouse, the south square room that was used as a sitting room and extension of the library, and two guest bedrooms: the north octagonal room with a then unusual built-in closet, and the north square room. Like other Monticello bedrooms, the guest bedrooms had alcove beds, beds set into the walls to provide more room space.

Library.   THOMAS JEFFERSON MEMORIAL FOUNDATION, INC./ JAMES TKATCH

Jefferson's bedroom.
THOMAS JEFFERSON MEMORIAL
FOUNDATION, INC./ JAMES TKATCH

49

Jefferson and his family entertained a continuous horde of visitors representing nearly all walks of American life. Some came for the day and left. Some came for the day and stayed a month or more. But disaster loomed as the former president realized his financial position was less than it should have been. Much of his financial undoing was traceable to his many years of public service that allowed him little time to attend to his personal affairs and those of the Monticello cash-producing farms. The rebuilding of Monticello had drained some of his resources. His constant entertaining had become a burdensome expense. The southern economy of the young United States—an agricultural economy based on slavery—was in bad circumstances. Jefferson's situation was so depressing that in April, 1826 his friends tried to gain hard cash by offering parcels of Jefferson land in a lottery. It did not work. Little money was realized. Nevertheless, other friends raised

Jefferson lottery ticket, 1826.
THOMAS JEFFERSON MEMORIAL FOUNDATION, INC.

Isaac Jefferson, a Jefferson slave and the manager of the Monticello nailery.
MANUSCRIPTS DEPARTMENT,
UNIVERSITY OF VIRGINIA LIBRARY

enough money to allow eighty-three-year-old Jefferson to live out his last days at Monticello, saving the property from his creditors.

Two months later, on July 4, 1826, the bright and extraordinary life of Thomas Jefferson ended. It was the fiftieth anniversary of the adoption of the Declaration of Independence. He was buried in the family burial ground not far from the mansion that was so much a part of his being and that he had designed almost sixty years earlier. A year later Jefferson's slaves and most of the mansion's furnishings were sold at auction to pay off creditors. By 1831 the empty mansion and some five hundred acres were sold to a Virginian, James Turner Barclay. Barclay sold the property three years later to a New York admirer of Thomas Jefferson, Lieutenant Uriah P. Levy of the United States Navy. Lieutenant Levy, who did not live full-time at Monticello, planned to preserve Jefferson's

home as a monument to the third president. He buried his mother, Rachel Phillips Levy, not far from the south pavilion and willed Monticello to the American people. But the government gave up its claim. Levy's heirs wrestled over the ownership of Monticello for seventeen years following his death in 1862.

Meanwhile, the property had been leased to a farmer who made a shambles of the grounds and mansion. The estate slipped into further disrepair when it was taken over by the Confederate Government during the Civil War. When the war ended, a seedy Monticello was returned to the Levy family who fought over control of the property.

In 1879 Uriah's nephew, Jefferson Monroe Levy, became the sole owner of the run-down estate. He immediately tried to restore Monticello to its original condition, thinking, perhaps, that one day the Federal Government would honor his

$35,000 in part discharge of it. There is, therefore, at this time, the sum of $72,000, remaining unpaid, to pay which, the lands of Mr. Jefferson are now offered for sale.

Valuable Lands for Sale.

The Lands of the Estate of THOMAS JEFFERSON, deceased, lying in the Counties of Campbell and Bedford, will be offered on the premises, if not previously sold privately, on Monday, the 22d of September next.

Likewise, MONTICELLO, in the County of Albemarle, with the Lands of the said estate adjacent thereto, including the Shadwell Mills, will be offered on the premises, if not previously sold privately, on Monday, the 29th of September next. The whole of this property will be devided to suit purchasers. The sale being made for the payment of the testator's debts, the desire to sell is sincere. The terms will be accommodating, and the prices anticipated low. Mrs. Randolph, of Monticello, will join in the conveyance, and will make the titles perfect.

TH. JEFFERSON RANDOLPH, Exec'r.
of THOMAS JEFFERSON, dec'd.

July 12, 1828.

Monticello land-sale notice, *Richmond Enquirer*, July 12, 1828.
THOMAS JEFFERSON MEMORIAL FOUNDATION, INC.

East front, circa 1870. MANUSCRIPTS DEPARTMENT,
UNIVERSITY OF VIRGINIA LIBRARY

East front, circa 1870.   MANUSCRIPTS DEPARTMENT, UNIVERSITY OF VIRGINIA LIBRARY

West front, circa 1870.

uncle's will and take over Jefferson's home on behalf of the American people. But despite his efforts, the years of neglect had nearly ruined the mansion and grounds. In 1900 Jefferson Monroe Levy began to live at Monticello during the summer months. His presence did much to prevent any vandalism and further deterioration of the property.

Finally, on April 13, 1923 the 180th anniversary of Thomas Jefferson's birth, the Thomas Jefferson Memorial Foundation was established to buy and preserve Monticello with the goal of making it a national monument. The Foundation purchased the mansion and six hundred acres surrounding it from Jefferson Monroe Levy for $500,000. The expense of purchase, maintenance, and recovering the original furnishings put off immediate meaningful restoration. It would take fifteen years of fund raising and planning before work could begin.

East front, circa 1870.   THOMAS JEFFERSON MEMORIAL FOUNDATION, INC.

East front, circa 1880.

West front and garden.

Major restoration of Monticello was under way by 1938. Two years later, the Garden Club of Virginia contributed funds to restore the gardens around the west and east porticos. In 1954 the mansion's structural elements were strengthened. Much of what had been the original mansion, its outbuildings, dependencies, and grounds were preserved and revived rather than rebuilt with new materials. Little by little the original Monticello began to appear inside and out as it had been when it was occupied by Thomas Jefferson and his family.

Monticello is not an ordinary place. It was the residence of one of the great historical figures in American history. It is an architectural expression steeped in traditions of elegance and learning. But more than these things, Monticello seems to hold the eternal presence of a rare and sensitive man who believed that "life, liberty, and the pursuit of happiness" is everyone's birthright.

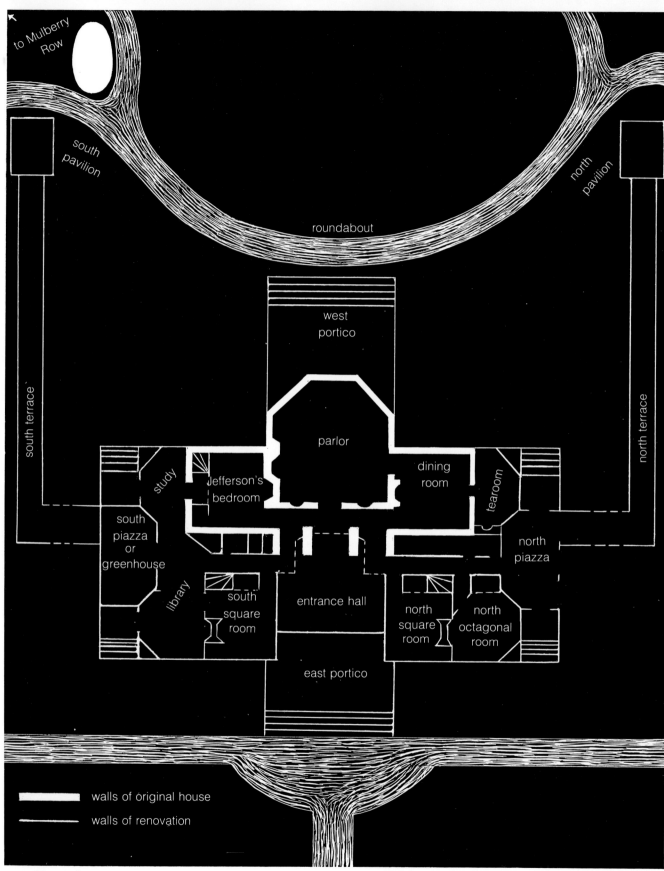

to Mulberry Row

south pavilion

north pavilion

roundabout

south terrace

north terrace

west portico

parlor

study

Jefferson's bedroom

dining room

tearoom

south piazza or greenhouse

library

south square room

entrance hall

north square room

north octagonal room

north piazza

east portico

walls of original house

walls of renovation

Floor plan. LEF

INDEX

(Italicized numbers indicate pages with photos.)

North pavilion, circa 1912.   THOMAS JEFFERSON MEMORIAL FOUNDATION, INC.

ACKNOWLEDGMENTS

Leonard Everett Fisher wishes to thank Lucia Stanton, Director of Research of the Thomas Jefferson Memorial Foundation, Charlottesville, Virginia, for her enthusiasm and guidance in researching this project; also, Millicent C. Travis and William L. Beiswanger, the Foundation's public affairs officer and architectural historian, respectively, for their special assistance.

Mr. Fisher would also like to thank the following organizations for granting permission to use photographs: Joseph Farber, page 26; The Massachusetts Historical Society, pages 10–11, 19 (top), 27 (bottom), 29; Museum of Fine Arts, Boston, page 9; The Thomas Jefferson Memorial Foundation, pages 2, 4–5, 6, 16–17, 18, 19 (bottom), 22–23, 31, 37, 38–39, 40, 41, 42, 43, 45, 46, 47, 48, 49, 50, 52, 57, 58–59, 60, 64; The University of Virginia Library, Manuscripts Department, page 27 (top), 51, 53, 54–55, 56; The University of Virginia Library, courtesy of the Rare Book Department, page 13.

Mr. Fisher took the photographs that appear on pages 1, 20, 21, 32, and the back of the jacket, and prepared the scratchboard drawings that appear on pages 24, 34, 41, 44 and 62.

Library of Congress Cataloging-in-Publication Data

Fisher, Leonard Everett.
Monticello.

Summary. Describes the planning, construction, and occupancy of Thomas Jefferson's dream home.
1. Monticello (Va.)—Juvenile literature.
2. Jefferson, Thomas, 1743–1826—Homes and haunts—Virginia—Juvenile literature.   [1. Monticello (Va.)
2. Jefferson, Thomas, 1743–1826—Homes and haunts]
I. Title
E332.74.F57   1988   973.4′6′0924   87-25219
ISBN 0-8234-0688-1